Wilderness Plots

Wilderness Plots

Tales About the Settlement of the American Land

by Scott R. Sanders

Illustrated by Dennis B. Meehan

William Morrow and Company, Inc.
New York   1983

SC
San

Earlier versions of these tales appeared in the following magazines:

Adena	*CoEvolution Quarterly*	*Georgia Review*
Carolina Quarterly	*Cream City Review*	*Indiana Writes*
Center	*December*	*Ohio Review*

Library of Congress Cataloging in Publication Data

Sanders, Scott R.
Wilderness plots.

1. Ohio River Valley—History—Fiction.   I. Title.
PS3569.A5137W5   1983   813'.54   83-7988
ISBN 0-688-02147-6

Printed in the United States of America

First Edition

1 2 3 4 5 6 7 8 9 10

BOOK DESIGN BY LINEY LI

TO RUTH

FOREWORD

These tales concern people who actually lived in the Ohio Valley, and events that actually occurred there, during the period of that valley's settlement—the period from the end of the Revolution in 1781 until the coming of the Civil War in 1861. But they are still *tales,* stories provoked by germs of fact, rather than history. When, in my reading, I turned up a character whose exploits or sufferings touched me, I wrote a narrative about him or her. Often I had no more than a sentence to work from, rarely more than a paragraph, because the people who appealed to me most were the obscure ones, whose names show up only in out-of-the-way chronicles, where they are recorded on account of some deed, some wildness, some quirk of personality. With one or two exceptions, I have not written about those people who are already famous in books. Instead I have written about the unmemorialized common folks, the carpenters and farmers, the fierce parents and moonstruck lovers, the sort of people who, in all ages, have actually made human history.

Thoreau went to Walden Pond to discover the truth

about nature, his own and that of the land on which he lived. He was convinced that if one studied any place deliberately enough, one could find out all there was worth knowing. I stop a good way short of that claim, for I have learned a great deal by traveling. But I have also learned a great deal by staying at home, and I am convinced that if one studies carefully the settlement of any region in America, one will discover the lineaments of our national character. Our ancestors wrestled with the land and its creatures for two and one half centuries before there were any cities or industries to speak of. We have all been shaped in part by that prolonged wrestling. I could have chosen someplace other than the Ohio Valley. But my feet know that place, so that is where I dig.

S.R.S
April 1983

CONTENTS

FINDING THE PLACE 15
GETTING THERE 18
SAVAGES 20
EMBRYO TOWN 22
THE COLD 24
AURORA MEANS DAWN 27
THE NAMING OF NAMES 29
CUTTING ROAD 31
LAW 34
THE CRIME OF POVERTY 36
LEARNING 38
FRUIT 40
HUNGER 42
SQUAW 45
FROSTBITE ON THE SOUL 47
BREACH OF THE SABBATH 50
CLEARING FOR SUNLIGHT 52
VOLUNTEER 54
THE INDIANS WIN ONE 57
PROFIT AND LOSS 60
HERMIT 62
SALT AND BULLETS 64
SPEAKER OF MANY TONGUES 66

THE VALUE OF AN OTTER'S HOLE 68

THE MULTIPLICATION OF WOOL 70

HUNT 72

WHAT THEY TOLD ABOUT THE BEASTS 75

THE INDIANS WIN ANOTHER ONE 77

THE CHARACTER OF HOGS 79

THE SWELLING AND SHRINKING OF THE WORLD 81

BONES 83

WHITE MAN'S GAME 85

OF TEETH AND TRANSPORTATION 88

LOVE-CROSSED CARPENTER 90

THE WANDERING OF LAKE ERIE 92

BORDER WAR 94

SLAVES NO MORE 96

COURTHOUSE 98

ICE MOUNTAINS AND HAIRY ELEPHANTS 101

THE BOY WHO NURSED CLEVELAND 103

THE PHILOSOPHICAL COBBLER 105

FREEING THE WATERS 107

BROKEN-BOOTED CANAL BUILDER 109

HEALING WATERS 112

SLANDER 114

THE INDIANS LOSE IT ALL 116

WITHOUT REGARD TO RACE 118

ONE OF THE UNION DEAD 121

AMERICA IS ONE LONG BLOODY FIGHT 123

THE MANNER OF THEIR DYING 125

"Here as well as anywhere I can look out my window and see the world. There are lights that arrive here from deep in the universe. A man can be provincial only by being blind and deaf to his province."—WENDELL BERRY

"This they tell, and whether it happened so or not I do not know; but if you think about it, you can see that it is true."—BLACK ELK

Wilderness Plots:

Plot: (1) a piece of ground marked off, set for a purpose, owned; (2) a chart or diagram; (3) a conspiracy; (4) the plan of action for a narrative.

FINDING THE PLACE

IT cost Robert Cavelier de La Salle $2,800 to discover the Ohio River. The Indians already knew where it was. You do not want to go there, they told La Salle. There are monsters in those waters ready to swallow you and your seven canoes. The wicked men who dwell on those shores will pull the arms from your body and suck the marrow from your bones.

La Salle had already sold everything but his coat and boots to finance the journey, so he was not going to be scared off by one tribe of savages warning him against another tribe. He took along two dozen men and three dozen muskets and a pair of priests. They paddled up the St. Lawrence, across Lake Ontario, and put in at a Seneca village near the mouth of the Genesee River. Having learned several Indian dialects in the leisure hours of his old trading-post days, La Salle was able to converse freely with his Seneca hosts. Do you know the great river to the west, he inquired, the one leading to the Sea of California and thence to China and Japan? They knew the great river

"One day his party glided into the elusive river."

that pours into the sea, yes. Would they lead him there? No, they answered, not for an armful of blankets.

After a month of fruitless hunting for guides, La Salle stumbled upon an Iroquois colony at the head of Lake Ontario. There he found a Shawnee prisoner who told him he could reach the great river in six weeks. Only six weeks? Fame was so close he could almost smell it. Eventually he turned up an Onondaga brave who was foolhardy enough to lead him.

By way of swamps, portages, and half the creeks in the territory, La Salle persevered in his journey to China. One day his party glided into the elusive river. Nothing in France could touch it for grandeur. In some places, herds of buffalo grazed in meadows that swept right down to the water. Brilliant green birds stitched the air with their singing.

After weeks of paddling, there was still no sign of the California Sea, let alone China. The falls at Louisville finally turned La Salle back, in 1669. He was not quite sure what he had discovered, nor where it led, nor what it was worth. But it was a considerable river. Oyo, he called it, garbling the Iroquoian word: Oyo, Ohio, beautiful river.

GETTING THERE

THE road to Ohio was strewn with many hazards. When he set out from his father's home in Exeter, during the autumn of 1789, Benjamin Bigsby thought New Hampshire was a wild place. But Vermont proved to be worse. The corduroy road hobbled one ox and loosened the joints of his cart. No sooner had he repaired the cart and rattled onward than he found that upstate New York was even worse, with all the rivers flooded and the Indians astir.

He built a raft to float one river, had to build another twelve miles farther on. The Indians he pacified with gifts of iron tools, keeping for himself only the froes and axes he would need to fashion a boat when he reached Lake Ontario, and to clear land when he reached Ohio. Snow began falling as he drove the last peg into his boat on Gerondaquet Bay.

By the time he reached the mouth of the Niagara, clinging to a shoreline barely visible through a blizzard, he found the river strangled with ice. Nothing he had been told about the falls prepared him for their murderous height or force. Poling his way upriver by shoving against blocks of ice, Bigsby watched the avalanche of water for half a day before he resigned himself to going ashore, dismantling the boat, and hauling it board by board (along with all his seed and tools) onto the plateau above the falls. While he tugged at the ropes, spray froze on his fingers and face. In his reassembled boat he poled his way to the mouth of Lake Erie, where a snowstorm drove him ashore once more.

When the weather cleared he picked his way through ice to Cleveland, which consisted of one log cabin at the mouth of the Cuyahoga River. The resident of Cleveland advised him that the river, where it was not frozen, was treacherous with rapids. Since Bigsby's land, bought from a speculator back in New Hampshire, lay seventeen miles farther inland, he left his goods in Cleveland and chopped a road across country. Once the road was cut, he recovered his goods, built a sled, and dragged all the seed and tools and dried food over the crusted snow to the clearing he had made on his own land, a place he named Endurance.

SAVAGES

THE first child born north of the Ohio River to white parents was a patriot before the fact, arriving in 1773 on the fourth of July, exactly three years before that date bore any uncommon weight on the calendar. The child was called John L. Roth, a name handed down from his father, who had not worn it out during all his journeys from Austria in the Old Country to this heathen Northwest Territory in the New.

Roth the elder had been kindled into evangelical flame in the faraway land of Moravia, and neither ocean crossing nor seven winters in the wilderness preaching among the Indians had quenched his fire. His message to the forest people was simple: shed no more blood, love one another, turn like children to Christ. By the time Roth the younger was born, the savages had become like ancient children. They had given up the skin houses in which they used to migrate like birds with the seasons. Now like white men they built log cabins, meaning to live rooted in the land as trees lived. As they buried fish in the hills of maize, so they planted their hearts in the soil of this one place.

They killed nothing with blood in it. Roth the younger was fed until his ninth year on plants and prayers. Then one day in that ninth year, the boy was climbing among the rafters in his father's lodge, searching for the spirit voices he heard up there, when along came a crowd of white men on horses. "Come out," the men shouted, "come out, we want to trade with you." And so the trusting children of Roth the elder, all except his only son by blood, shuffled into the ring of horses, muttering welcome in their acquired language. True to their learning they did not run or even raise their fists when the white men shot them down.

Roth the younger, first-born American in this territory, clung to the roof beam, listening.

EMBRYO TOWN

THE Governor of the Northwest had not returned, as scheduled, to the fort, whether on account of drinking or whoring no one could guess. In an effort to stave off anarchy, Jonathan Meigs took it upon himself to draft a code of laws, which he nailed to an elm tree:

No Wimmen Anywheres
No Fires Indoors
No Guns Under Beds
Not Much Licker
No Traffic With Injuns

By thrashing five soldiers personally, shackling three to the water wagon, and breaking the arm and collarbone, respectively, of two others, Meigs enforced his rules. At his command a canal was dug and lined with sandstone to carry water from the Killbuck River. He handled a shovel himself. Later, hefting an ax, he helped girdle trees for a clearing, where corn would grow for the soldiers and oats for the horses. He carried a pine-tar torch from stump to stump, lighting them. In the still air, trunks of smoke rose from every stump like a ghostly forest.

The men with keenest eyes Meigs sent out hunting for anything large with a skin around it, and those whose eyes were poor, the wasters of lead, he set to tanning hides and sewing breeches. Meigs himself peeled oak bark and gathered gall nuts for tanning, so he could keep an eye on the hunters in the woods and the tanners in the fort. He sent three men back over the Allegheny Mountains for a herd of sheep, which they were to steal if necessary, in order to supply his commonwealth with mutton and wool. While they were gone he planted flax so his men might wear linen mixed with their wool, and he set about building a loom from memory of his mother's.

Upon arrival at the fort, therefore, the Governor of the Northwest found no chaos, no hunger or cold, no lack of shelter—no need for him at all. Reading the signature at the bottom of the sheet of laws, the Governor promptly ordered six men to nail Jonathan Meigs by his jerkin to the elm, where he dangled beside his weather-stained legislation, as a warning to all would-be usurpers.

THE COLD

THE weeds at the head of Bone Creek were so tall and fierce that Hames Kingsbury decided he would settle there. Any soil capable of shooting green juice up through four feet of yarrow or thistle, he reasoned, would sprout good corn and wheat. Crops he would need, for he meant to winter through with his wife and his coming child. Others had settled there with the same determination, but each one had been chilled into leaving by the winter's advance of snow.

Once he settled, Kingsbury swore he would not shift ground again for ice or man or any power on earth. At summer's end he laid sickle to his wheat, the first man ever to do so in the territory, and he shelled his corn. Every grain passed between his fingers. During the fall, while he banked leaves against his house and split the wood he had gathered in summer, one by one the other folks withdrew, the tanners with their bark, the masons with their loads of stone, the few farmers of corn with their carts of whiskey. By the first snow Kingsbury and his wife were as lonely as people could be on this earth.

". . . as he was the first white child born, he was
the first to die, in the sixtieth day of snow."

When the child was born, a boy, the snow stood four feet at the door. They would wait until spring to name him.

After thirty-eight days of snow, which Kingsbury counted by notching a stick, the rabbits and squirrels and rats found the grain, scrabbling into the cabin at night, made bold by hunger. Kingsbury beat them off with a stick all night, his wife shooed them all day, but still the corn dwindled, the wheat vanished altogether, and the snow froze harder. When the wife's milk failed they tried feeding the child corn mush and rabbit broth, but he curled his back and refused. And so, as he was the first white child born in Pilgrim County, he was the first to die, starving to death in the sixtieth day of snow.

AURORA MEANS DAWN

WHEN Job Sheldon reached Ohio in 1800, with family, wagon, and yoke of oxen, he was greeted by one hellacious thunderstorm. The children wailed. Mrs. Sheldon spoke of returning to Connecticut. The oxen pretended to be stone outcroppings, and would budge neither forward nor backward for all of Sheldon's thwacking. Lightning toppled so many oaks and elms across the wagon track, in any case, that even a dozen agreeable oxen would have done them no good.

They camped. More precisely, they spent the night squatting in mud beneath the wagon, trying to keep dry. Mrs. Sheldon kept saying there had never been any storms even remotely like this one back in Connecticut. Nor any cheap land, her husband added. No land's cheap if you perish before setting eyes on it, she said. And that ended talk for the night. Every few minutes, Mrs. Sheldon would count the children, touching each head in turn, to make sure none of the seven had vanished in the deluge.

Next morning it was hard to tell just where the wagon track had been, there were so many trees down. Sheldon tried cutting his way forward. After a mile, however, and seven felled trees, he decided to fetch help from Aurora, their destination. On the land-company map which Sheldon had carried from the East, Aurora was advertised as a village, with mill and store and clustered cabins. But the actual place turned out to consist of a surveyor's post, topped by a red streamer. So he walked to the next village shown on the map—Hudson—which fortunately did exist, and there he found eight men who agreed to help him clear the road.

Their axes flashed for hours in the sunlight before they reached the wagon. The children huddled in shirts while their outer garments dried on nearby bushes. Mrs. Sheldon sat fully dressed and shivering. With the track cleared, the oxen still could not move the wagon through mud until everyone piled out and the nine men put shoulders to the wheels. Even though they reached Aurora after nightfall, making out the surveyor's post in lantern light, the eight axmen insisted on returning immediately to their own homes. The blades glinted on their shoulders as they disappeared from the circle of the campfire.

Dry at last, Job Sheldon carried his lantern through this forest that would be his farm. Aurora meant dawn, he knew that. And his family was the dawn of dawn, the first glimmering in this new place. The next settlers did not come for three years.

THE NAMING OF NAMES

EXCEPT for barbaric Indian words, which did not count, the map of Ohio was as bald of names when the first white people settled there as it had been on the day of creation. Without titles for the creeks and swamps and hills, nobody could be sure where they were when they arrived somewhere.

When Josiah Hubbard got swept away and drowned and thoroughly mangled by a swollen stream, that place became Breakneck Creek. And so other places became Rattlesnake Knob, Black Bottom Swamp, Mad River, Put-in-Bay, Killbuck.

A two-cabin clearing was called Swamptown, on account of the boggy land. Then a bear carried off one of the babies, and it was called Beartown. Then Israel Thorndike offered to donate an acre for a town square, and the place was renamed Thorndike. After he reneged on his offer, the place was retitled in honor of its five major landholders, one after another, as each outbid the previous one with offers of free land. Finally the name settled down to Brimfield, after the chief landholder's home county back in Massachusetts.

And so other clearings were named for homeplaces back in New England, which had been named for homeplaces back in Old England: London, Cambridge, Lancaster, Somerset. Most of the ancient world was represented somewhere on the Ohio map: Troy, Athens, Lebanon, Paris, Palmyra, Delphi, Sparta, Mecca. Trees and fruits and beasts donated names: Beaver Creek, Locust Grove, Cherry Valley, Sunfish River.

Asked to name the village into which she had just moved, Widow Amariah Wheelock called it Freedom, to signify that she and most of her new neighbors had escaped debts or jail terms by settling there. And so other villages were called Enterprise, Mount Hope, Defiance, Recovery, Twenty Mile Stand, Morning Sun. In exchange for donating a barrel of whiskey to support a church-raising, Charles Curtiss had a hamlet named after him, Charlestown. The settlement that grew up around Heman Ely's tavern became Elyria. The name of Moses Cleaveland, surveyor from Connecticut, lost a letter and became Cleveland when it was attached to a clearing on Lake Erie. And so were many places named, after men ranging from surveyors to Presidents, from barkeeps to generals: Napoleon, Cincinnati, Adams, Washington, Jefferson.

But for all their struggle to imprint their own names on the Ohio wilderness, the white settlers could not eradicate the Indian words. Those haunting syllables crept back out of the soil, sang in the rivers: Miami, Ottawa, Pickawillany, Chillicothe, Cuyahoga, Tuscarawas, Shenandoah, Ohio.

CUTTING ROAD

EBENEZER Zane's secret was having seven grown sons, each of whom owned an ax and gazed at the world with the eyes of a dreamer. His own eyes had a habit of turning forest into tilled field, seeing roads march through swamps. He could look at stony land and imagine it channeled by canals. Believing in neither rock nor tree root because they were hidden beneath the soil, Zane envisioned plows cutting meadows that other men had abandoned.

Magical eyesight, his wife called it, this power of seeing a breakneck countryside turned to human purposes, and she said so without any humor. She was one who always saw the buried rocks and tree roots, always smelled a skim of sweat on any field that people had cleared. She had given up protesting aloud, since her sons, like her husband, stalked out of the house whenever she challenged their harebrained schemes, and now she generally hammered her rage into bread dough or cornmeal. But when she heard about the plan for a government bridle path, she let out a howl.

"His own eyes had a habit of seeing roads . . ."

She found all eight men squatting in the shade, passing whetstones from hand to hand, sharpening their axes. "What are you fixing to do, Eben?" Looking up from his honing, but without bringing his eyes to focus on her despairing face, Zane answered: "Chop a bridle path for the government from the Ohio River at Wheeling across the Territory to Chillicothe, and then down to Limestone in Kentucky." "And how many hundred miles of chopping is that?" she demanded. "I won't know till I walk it," he said.

They did walk it, and chop it too, never seeing the trees before them but always an open path. They camped wherever the previous day's ax work had led them. They rose each morning to wrap callused hands around the hickory handles. They swung the blades in time to songs Ebenezer sang.

The government, repaying his labors with a grant of four hundred acres, now could send marshals and justices on horseback deeper into the wilderness on his bridle path. Because of Zane and his seven sons with their visionary eyes, the mails soon opened through his path their seepage of letters.

LAW

CHICKENS, dried apples, maple sugar, corn dodgers, and ripe whiskey suffered considerably when the circuit judge and his attendant lawyers passed through town. If Asa D. Keyes was among the lawyers, the whiskey supply was not likely to recover anytime soon. He surely could put it away. On occasion the influence showed.

Keyes himself liked to recollect the time he hired a horse from Judge Amzi Atwater to ride to Warren. Upon returning, Keyes explained to the judge that he believed the bridle had been changed. "Yes," said Judge Atwater, "and the horse, too—that is a better animal than the one I let you have." It turned out that Keyes and a Squire Tyler of Hubbard had been imbibing pretty freely all day, and on leaving Warren each had mounted the other's horse. Too full of spirits to unriddle their mistake, the two rode home upon swapped horses.

Despite his intemperate habits, Keyes was appointed U.S. attorney for the Ninth Judicial Circuit of Ohio. He rode horseback with the judge from county seat to county seat, prosecuting folks for everything from sedition to tampering with the mails. Between trials he stayed afloat on a tide of whiskey.

The drinking gave him little pleasure, but it helped him forget how thin the crust of law was in this godforsaken region. In some counties the judge would sentence a criminal to jail, then let him go because there was no jail. In other counties the court would sit in somebody's parlor, or under a tree, or in the loft of a barn. Elsewhere the court could not sit at all, for fear of getting shot up by local people who preferred settling their disputes in the old muscular fashion.

Maps would tell you Ohio was a state, the same as Virginia was. But Indians and British spies and roughnecks of every stripe belied the maps. In 1804 Ohio was a governmental fiction imposed upon wilderness, an act of imagination. Traveling the bridle paths with his judge, Asa Keyes felt the crust quaking beneath him. Someday the entire populace might drop through it into barbarism. Fear of that plunge kept him drinking.

THE CRIME OF POVERTY

U NLIKE the cells for murderers, the cells for debtors were provided with iron-barred windows. Through his grating Gallipolis Jennings could watch the goings-on of his fellow citizens who were fortunate enough not to have been sullied by the crime of poverty. His own poverty had been honestly arrived at, with the benefit of every calamity you would care to mention, including a mud slide and a bank failure. His family boarded with neighbors while he studied the grain in the timbers of his cell.

Creditors occasionally stopped by to chat with him on the subject of money. But how was a man to conjure silver coins out of thin air? First he borrowed a spinning wheel from the sheriff's wife, thinking he could buy his way out of debt with yarn. But even after his fingers grew deft at the work, he calculated he would still need upwards of nine years of spinning to clear himself. Next he tried candle making, and that cut the time down to seven years. Clearly he would have to find work outside, or he would turn to mold before paying his debts.

He signed his plow, wagon, and horses over to the creditors as security, for which sacrifice he was allowed to spend the daylight hours outside jail. But he was never allowed to wander farther than four hundred and forty yards in any direction from his cell. Even at that he was lucky, the sheriff explained, because back in 1799 the boundary had been set at only two hundred yards. "That's a piece of English law I could live without," Jennings replied. "Just see you obey it," said the sheriff.

Four hundred and ten yards from the jail was a saddle-maker who agreed to hire Jennings—but at a bargain wage, in view of his criminal status. In 1805 the prison bounds were reduced by federal statute to four hundred yards. So Jennings had to hunt a closer job. His wife and children moved back to Rhode Island. His horses aged in the paddocks of his creditors.

He learned blacksmithing, laboring the first six months without pay on account of his inexperience. When the blacksmith moved his shop to a brick building some five hundred yards from the jail, beyond the legal limit, Gallipolis Jennings took advantage of a moonless night to quit Ohio altogether, and go see what Indiana had to offer in the way of employment.

LEARNING

IT galled Smither Mahowald, who fled Ireland in 1798 after the failure of his country's revolt against England, to have to teach Ohio children mathematics in terms of pounds, shillings, and pence. Damn the king's money! But the only arithmetic book approved by the school trustees was English.

What more could you expect of a backwoods settlement whose promise of payment read as follows: "Agreed with Smither Mahowald, of Pilgrim County, formerly of County Sligo, Ireland, to teach school in Roma three months, for twelve bushels of wheat per month; one-half to be paid at the end of three months in grain, and the remainder in some other trade, such as cattle, sheep, and whiskey." Any trustee who could so neatly translate wheat into sheep would experience no difficulty ciphering in shillings and pence.

Smither Mahowald therefore taught King George's arithmetic, hating the fat tyrant all the while. For reading, there were the King James version of the Bible and the splendiferous *Columbian Orator,* the latter featuring speeches by English sea captains and members of Parliament. At least the speller was American, by Mr. Noah Webster of Massachusetts.

To tell the truth, Mahowald would rather have been paid in the king's silver, just so it *be* silver, than in wheat or cows. The money you could shove in your pocket and carry away, to someplace less barbarous than Roma, Ohio. But you could expect no silver of any kind out here, where money was so scarce a man would often make change by sawing a coin into quarters with his knife.

Three months of schooling was all the citizens could afford in 1806, so that was all he taught, from the first of December until the first of March, boarding each week with a different family. All day long he paced the slab-log floor, staring over the shoulders of thirty-two reluctant scholars. The children sat on puncheon trestles, ranked according to their ages from four years to twenty-one. Their hullabaloo rattled the clay chinks between the schoolhouse logs and loosened the hair on Mahowald's head. Parents advised him to thrash the unruly ones. But he had seen enough violence in Ireland—where his own people were considered the unruly ones—to cure him of any desire for thrashing. Instead, he gritted his teeth and tried gentleness, which worked passably well. Perhaps, as the proverb said, an elephant really could be led by a hair, a child by kindness.

FRUIT

THE gravest mistake the Indians made was suffering any white man who had once viewed their plantation to escape with his tongue in his head. They set the spy free, thinking that word of their might would frighten the army away. But when the raggedy spy arrived panting at the commander's feet to describe the acres of peaches and apples, of beans and maize, General Anthony Wayne rose to saddle his horse, knowing he had found at last the Indians' soft belly. Stab them there, hard, and their will to resist the advance of white men would bleed away.

Wayne rode the bounds of his encampment, rousing his army with promises of fresh fruit at the end of the next day's fighting. All night, under the linsey-woolsey tents, men dreamed of boughs clustered with apples, heavy with peaches, and Wayne dreamed among them. This was no phantom city of gold, such as the Spaniards had stumbled after in the West; this was something altogether more valuable—fertile land already cleared of forest and broken for the plow.

In the morning, when he glimpsed from a neighboring

hill the mosaic of Indian gardens, saw the pruned or-
chards, the black earth streaked by rows of green, when he
traced the web of ditches and footpaths, Wayne debated
for several minutes whether to invade such an orderly
place. But the men shuffled restlessly behind him, with
visions of fruit in their heads.

We can tend this plantation with as much husbandry as
the Indians have shown, the general told himself. Yet as
he raised his arm in signal to advance, as he watched the
first soldiers trample through the rows of beans, their
shoulders catching on the lower limbs of apple trees,
Wayne had second thoughts. After his victory, which the
army celebrated by tearing laden boughs from the or-
chard, settlers called the place Defiance.

HUNGER

WHEN George Haymaker built his gristmill on Bone Creek he had no idea how much hunger lurked in the backwoods. As word of his building seeped through the countryside, men materialized to help him wrestle the grindstones into place, mount the waterwheel, channel the creek. Before he had even laid a roof on the crotched poles that served for walls, the men were back with their bags of corn. While Haymaker fed grain between the swirling grindstones, the settlers told of children back home with bellies swollen by hunger; they told of being overtaken by nightfall on the trail, of being chased by wolves.

At sundown Haymaker was relieved by his miller, who kept the stones grinding by lantern light. All night Haymaker dreamed the sounds of wooden gears meshing, water rushing, stones rasping; waking from nightmares of starving babies he heard the actual sounds of the mill, grinding through the darkness.

When the creek began to freeze, men hammered the young ice with clubs to keep the water flowing. But when

"Standing in the door of his mill watching them
come with their bulging gunny sacks ..."

the creek finally froze hard as a trough of glass, the settlers holed up in their cabins, pounding their corn and wheat with mallets, using fire-hollowed stumps for mortars. When thaws came, if the mill was not swept away by floods, it was so thronged with settlers, each one bearing his sack of corn, that many were forced to camp out for several days while awaiting their turn.

Pained by all this hunger, Haymaker added a second pair of stones, then a third; he cut a channel to Flimsy Creek so he might have more waterpower. And still the hungry trooped to the mill, on ox sled or muleback if they were lucky, more often on foot. Standing in the door of his mill, watching them come with their bulging gunnysacks slung over shoulders, Haymaker imagined the wilderness as a gigantic maw, swallowing every scrap of food that men and women could raise, and bellowing for more.

SQUAW

TIRING of his squaw, who fed his supper to the dogs if he was half a minute late in sitting down, Jonathan Alder yearned for white people. Besides, she never washed, and at night she crept out to join the sweaty dancing. Alder was not overclean himself, but that was a matter for his own nose.

From the day when she found him in Gutty Swamp with his leg broken and dragged him home, slung upon her rawhide dress, herself going naked, she had always done whatever she took it into her mind to do. If she wanted to hunt bear, she would go hunt bear, leaving him three days with no one to cook his food or wash his feet. If she did not want to hear what he was saying, she would clap hands over her ears and turn away.

To tame her, he decided to marry her. But the ceremony had to wait eleven days because she was fasting on a hilltop. When she descended, and succumbed to the ritual, her eyes were more flighty than ever. As a wife she was even more wayward, sleeping through the day and staying up all night to chant, piling rotted scraps of food on the floor. In the midst of making love she would slip into trances and narrate visions from worlds that had nothing to do with Jonathan Alder. She was too strong to beat, too dreamy to shout into obedience.

So the next spring Alder began thinking tenderly of his wife back in the white settlement. On the night he chose to desert his squaw, she left him first, stalking into the hills with frenzied eyes. His own wife welcomed him back by cooking him breakfast, saying nothing of the seven months gone by since he had vanished in search of muskrats into Gutty Swamp. She had reckoned he would turn up. His children soon knew him again, and hung about his knees. And the minister, asked in secret about the marriage to the squaw, advised him that it meant nothing, since it was an Indian ceremony, of no consequence to God.

FROSTBITE ON THE SOUL

REVEREND Shadrack Bostwick was a physician of souls and boots. He would as soon mend a broken shoe as exorcize demons, for who could ponder on God while limping footsore over stony ground? Rising at three on a Sunday, he would ride from church to puny church, preaching an hour in every one, to congregations of nine and thirteen. Faith was spread thin in that place. The bodies of his listeners sucked strength from him, so they could return to their cabins for another week of battling the land, while he returned to his own cabin after midnight as limp as frostbitten grass.

During the week he ruminated upon his sermons while making shoes. The business of cutting shapes from leather, molding them around a last, and stitching them together into a shoe seemed to Bostwick a humble imitation of God's own creation. For what was the body but a vessel for the soul, as a boot was the vessel for a foot?

In his sermons he often spoke of God the cobbler. He would hold a shoe aloft, with his hand stuffed inside, and declare this clumsy contrivance to be a token of our

47

"During the week he ruminated upon his
sermons while making shoes."

fleshly body. Then he would withdraw his hand, wriggling the fingers which could carve wood or sew stitches, could heal or wound, could do in fact anything a man was capable of imagining, and this he declared an image of the soul. His listeners nodded. They could feel the difference between flesh and leather. They could believe in a cobbler God. And so Bostwick sowed the word in the wilderness.

One January Sunday in 1807 his mare broke her leg in a woodchuck hole. After shooting her, the minister continued afoot through snowdrifts to his next church, eight frozen miles away. By the time he arrived his feet were numb with frostbite. No amount of stamping would bring feeling back to them, no roasting by the fire nor dry socks would warm them. From that morning onward, Bostwick never spoke of the foot inside its boot as an image of the soul inside its body without feeling a sense of terror at his own numbness.

BREACH OF THE SABBATH

THE judges chewed their moustaches in irritation.
Here they were, ready to begin the very first sitting
of the Court of Common Pleas in Pilgrim County, and
the house where they were to have presided was burned to
a cinder. William Simcox was suspected of the arson. But
what could anyone prove?

Since it was a warm day, the judges held court beside
the smoking ruins, in the shade of a tulip tree. In the
morning they swore in a grand jury, appointed trustees
for the local dead, settled land disputes, and heard several
suits for debt. Echoes from the gavel rattled off the slate
banks of the Pickawillany River.

Following a dinner-time adjournment, the afternoon
sessions began. Having been instructed by the prosecutor
during their pork and sweet potatoes, the grand jury
brought in two indictments against William Simcox, one
for larceny and the other for breach of the Sabbath. No
mention was made of the arson. According to the larceny
charge, Simcox had shot a tame deer, valued at $3, be-
longing to Moses Pond, and afterward had dragged the

carcass to his home. Since one of the judges had been along with him when he did the shooting, Simcox pleaded guilty to that.

According to the second charge, on the fifth of June, 1808, Simcox "wickedly and maliciously interrupted, molested and disturbed the religious society of Euphrates Township while meeting, assembled, and returning from divine worship, by sporting and hunting game with guns and hounds." That Simcox denied. "You never ran your hounds outside the meeting hall, nor fired off your gun beside the doorway?" one of the judges inquired. "Sure I did," Simcox answered, "but it wasn't malicious, on account of I never knew it was Sunday. I don't keep no calendar." For his sacrilegious ignorance, Simcox was fined a day's labor on the public highway, and made to recite the days of the week five hundred times in the presence of the sheriff.

CLEARING FOR SUNLIGHT

AS a veteran of the Revolution, Ethelbert Baker was granted one hundred acres of land in the Western Reserve. After walking to Ohio from Virginia, where the war had finished with him, only to find that the land he had been deeded was entirely swamp, Baker returned in bitterness to his home in Connecticut.

Those who had made money from the Revolution soon formed the Connecticut Land Company, which bought Palmyra Township in Portage County. As an inducement to its settlement, these gentlemen gave Baker one hundred acres of land to go there, make a clearing, and build a cabin—which he accordingly did. Before leaving, however, he warned the shareholders that if the land turned out to be more swamp, he would come back and carve them up.

The land proved to be hardwood forest. While feeding himself on acorn bread and rabbits during the first season, Baker managed to clear enough land for a planting of corn and wheat. At his first harvest he gathered over a bushel of wheat. He threshed the grain by hand and carried it on his shoulders to Poland, about thirty miles away, there had it milled, and returned with it to his cabin. Raccoons devoured the corn. All that fall and winter he chopped trees, pushing the forest back from his cabin, and the next spring he planted a larger field of grain.

At the second harvest he gathered more wheat than he could carry on his shoulders, so he built a cart with wheels cut cross-grain from the stumps of gum trees. And so each year, hungry for bare dirt and sunlight, he enlarged the tear in the forest, and each year he hauled more wheat to Poland for grinding. By the outbreak of war with England in 1812, he owned two wagons and four oxen, had built his own mill on Slippery Creek and his own still for turning corn into whiskey. The new settlers elected him justice of the peace.

All this was a good deal to abandon in order to fight in the war against England, on behalf of a country that had awarded him one hundred acres of swamp for fighting in the Revolution. But Baker fought, and at the Battle of the Thames near Detroit he died.

VOLUNTEER

"**Y**OU'RE free to stay here with the women and children and cripples," Captain Shaler told the regiment, "or you can volunteer to defend the frontier against the English." The drum and fife band played louder than the gears of a waterwheel. "We need fifty brave men," said the captain, "fifty patriots to go join General Hull at Detroit." First to step out and join the musicians was Samuel Redfield, next came Alva Day, then quickly several others, all of them marching back and forth to the music.

Grant Redden was pretending to be somewhere else— in his smokehouse or his privy—anywhere but among these ranked militiamen who were being called upon to enlist for war. He did not even know for sure where Detroit was.

"Fifty, we need fifty heroes," the captain kept shouting. The musicians kept drumming and tooting. Redden kept slumping lower in the ranks of the uncommitted. Every time the volunteers marched past him, their familiar eyes asked the same question—How about you?

Finally the total reached forty-nine, and Grant Redden still held onto his freedom like a bear trap on a bear. "There's a star down by the horizon," the captain declared. "Visible in daylight! Star of promise!" Redden could barely stand the fife and drum. An astronomical portent was one item too many. "Show me any damned daytime star," he shouted, "and I'll join!"

Captain Shaler pointed. Redden stared long and long. He wouldn't admit the star was actually there until half the regiment announced that they could see it as clear as anything.

So Redden was enrolled. Like the others, he ate turkey pie at the Independence Day supper for volunteers. He listened to the Congregational preacher invoking an American God on July 5. Then like the others he walked to Cleveland, came down with diarrhea in Sandusky, slept under tents made from homespun linen sheets, suffered dread and seasickness on the sail across Lake Erie. At the mouth of the Raisin River, the boat had to blunder for hours among the bullrushes in search of a channel.

No sooner was the regiment landed, however, than a British officer arrived with news that Hull had already surrendered his own troops and in addition all of those, including Redden's garrison, who were on their way to Detroit. Thanks therefore to one of the most liberal surrenders in the annals of warfare, Redden was soon on his way back to Ohio aboard a British ship. When he reached home no stars were visible on the horizon, day or night. Of the fifty who had volunteered, twelve died of fever and ague, three from eating a heifer poisoned by Indians, one of drowning in Put-in-Bay, and not a single man of them had fired a shot.

THE INDIANS WIN ONE

WIDOW Whittaker's claim that an Indian had stolen her horse was a blessing and a curse to the soldiers of Fort Sandusky. Instead of fighting the British, as they had volunteered to do, the Fourth Brigade of the Fourth Division of the Ohio Militia were digging a well. After a week's shoveling, the hole was twenty-eight feet deep and dry as a year-old gourd.

When the Indian charged with horse thieving was caught, therefore, the entire brigade recommended that he be put down the hole for safekeeping. This made sense to Godfrey Varnum, Indian agent for the territory. (He was also son of the Speaker of the United States House of Representatives, which explains how he became an Indian agent.) So the accused was put down the well and the soldiers were given a recess from digging. That was the blessing.

Presently, Varnum held a council with the Indians at Seneca Town, where it was agreed that the prisoner would be returned in exchange for Widow Whittaker's horse and a good dressed beef. Both sides smoked to that. The

"The entire Brigade recommended that he be put down the hole for safe keeping."

horse was bedraggled with burdock seeds, but otherwise unmarked. The Indian was hoisted from the well and set on his way. The soldiers' only compensation for the renewed digging was the prospect of a beef dinner. After months of bread and salt pork, the plump heifer delivered by the Indians looked more enticing than the golden calf of the Israelites. Widow Whittaker cooked it. The brigade devoured it. Then came the curse.

Before dawn half the garrison were retching from atop the twelve-foot pickets of the fort, and the other half were groaning on their beds of hazel bushes. Only Godfrey Varnum, who preferred mutton to beef, and who came from a Massachusetts family rich enough to afford the choice, had refused to dine on the heifer. Only Varnum felt like walking to Seneca Town. Poison? the Indians answered with blank faces. Poison our gift beef? Never! But who can say what locoweed a calf will eat in the meadows?

The Fourth Brigade held a contest for slowness of recovery, since nobody was eager to resume digging the well. Eventually the shoveling was resumed, and at thirty-one feet, just a yard below where the prisoner had stood, they hit water.

PROFIT AND LOSS

UPON hearing that provisions were fetching a high price at the military camp near Wooster, Daniel Cross set out for that point in December 1812 with one son and a wagonload of oats. That first sale doubled his worldly wealth. Because horse teams were so scarce, Cross then signed on for high wages to transport the camp's baggage to Mansfield. At Mansfield they induced him with yet higher wages to continue on to Fort Sandusky. Finally at Sandusky he was paid off, and he headed back home to Roma. Along the way he bought four oxen and seventeen steers, for resale to his neighbors. Avenues to wealth yawned before him.

Wagon, herd, son, and Daniel Cross rumbled back through Wooster on the eighth of January. Soon after they trudged into the valley of Killbuck River, there came on a fearful snowstorm, which lasted three days. Cross and son vanished into history.

His wife sent another son to hunt them. When he also failed to return, she sent yet a third son, who was shrewd enough to assemble the settlers of Wooster into a search party. Three miles up the valley of the Killbuck they found Cross's skull and a few of his bones picked clean by wolves. Beside him in the snow lay his opened jackknife and shreds of his buckskin hunting shirt. The remains of four oxen, still in yoke, were found nearby, where they had been chained to a tree. No trace of the lost sons or of the father's overnight wealth was ever found.

From time to time in the following spring one of Cross's seventeen steers, haggard and jerky-eyed, would mosey into Wooster. The bones of the unfortunate seller of oats were gathered up and buried in a field just south of Lodi, and his name was carved upon a beech-tree in Killbuck Valley. His wife kept the jackknife.

HERMIT

ELEVEN miles south of Chillicothe, on a cliff over-looking the river, lived the hermit of the Scioto. Boatmen heaving their way upstream with poles or drifting lazily down would see him squatting on a ledge, the throat of a cave gaping behind him. He would answer no shouted greeting. Whatever the time of day, he would be staring directly into the sun, with eyes that looked from the river as if they had been drilled into his head.

Tales grew up around him, as they clustered around every grotesque tree and boulder on the river. According to one yarn he was a half-breed abandoned in the cave by white and red man alike, nursed through infancy by wolves. Wolf milk was easy to believe, because the hermit looked shaggy and ferocious, white hair blown in a mane about his head like a dandelion gone to seed, beard thick as moss clinging to his chest, and those eyes like sockets bored into rock.

No one had ever heard him make more noise than the limestone cliffs, no one even believed he could speak, until one day a party of ministers on their way to Chillicothe paddled their black-coated bodies up the river beneath his cave. For the half hour they spent toiling past, rehearsing the wolf tale, they could see his head turning to follow the sun. When they had paddled almost beyond earshot he suddenly leapt to his feet and screamed at them in a fierce unintelligible language.

The ministers stared at each other, and then back at the hermit, who had squatted again in silence upon his ledge. They agreed not to speak of this incident in Chillicothe, for fear people would gather at the cliff and prod the hermit into mad sermons. Even if his words seemed nonsense, they might possess magical powers and might work upon the soul unawares.

SALT AND BULLETS

BECAUSE his father's house was fortified, Joseph Vance came to know all the neighbors, who scurried there in time of troubles. Troubles there were aplenty, from white brigands and Indians and beasts, so neighbors spent a good deal of time firing muskets and curses between slits in the log walls. Watching them as a child, Vance observed two things—their love of guns and their need for salt.

By the time he turned fifteen in 1796, he had earned enough from plowing and woodchopping to buy himself a yoke of oxen, a wagon, and seven barrels of salt, with which he set out on a speculative tour through the settlements. Everywhere he went people bought his salt. But each settled clearing in the woods was separated from the next by hours of thickets, days of swamp, and flooded rivers. Bones showed through the oxen's hides. Vance himself grew stony about the eyes. During the day he hacked his way through briars, or waited beside swollen rivers for the waters to fall. By night he fed huge fires to terrify the wolves and panthers, and caught snatches of sleep on the ground beside his oxen. Occasionally a mountain lion would brave the fire to creep into camp, and Vance would rouse from sleep to shoot it.

He persevered. Wherever he drove his salt, he carved his name into doorposts. When his seven barrels were empty he bought land upon Mad River, but kept aside enough money to buy seven more barrels of salt and seven of lead, with which he set out again upon his speculative rounds. He found that people would buy rifle balls and salt even when they lacked shoes. After each journey he acquired more land.

For such a man it was an easy matter to get elected captain of a rifle company at age twenty-three, lead men against the Indians in the War of 1812, become supplier to the Northwestern army in 1817. People who remembered his steadfast eyes above the gaunt oxen, his cup filled with salt, his name upon the doorpost, elected him to the state legislature, and then to Congress, and then in his sixty-fourth year to the governorship. In every office he served shrewdly.

SPEAKER OF MANY TONGUES

THAT Reuben Root had preserved his life at all was a remarkable fact, upon which he would gladly comment in any of four ancient languages. Root had moved as a boy from his native Vermont to Canada, where he received a classical education, which peopled his mind with antique heroes.

When the Canadian authorities drafted him to fight against the Americans in 1812, he refused, not wanting to oppose his own fatherland. One stormy night he escaped, keeping the antique heroes before his imagination—Odysseus and Aeneas and all the lesser ones—as he paddled across Lake Ontario in a birchbark canoe. Night settled about him blacker than the robes of ministers. By and by the storm cast him up half drowned upon an island. There he was stranded for three days, chewing on his belt to still the gnawing in his belly. When at last he reached Sacket's Harbor (his canoe filled to the gunwales with water), he was arrested by an American patrol who took him to be a spy.

He would soon have been locked away if an uncle,

hearing about the arrest, had not showed up to vouch for his loyalty. Upon his release, Root proceeded to Vermont, raised a company of men, and was elected captain. They marched to the northern frontier, where they fought in the battles of Plattsburg and Lake Champlain. Root himself kept thinking of Greek and Phoenician campaigns. Once the battles were won and the company disbanded, he trained himself in the law.

In 1818—possessed now of a wife, an infant daughter, and a silver quarter of a dollar—he moved to the village of Cleveland, which he imagined might become an Athenian city upon the shore of Lake Erie. As judge on the Court of Common Pleas, and later as justice upon the Supreme Court, he preserved this vision of a heroic city rising in the heart of the country. In his own garden he planted olive trees, which froze, and grapevines, which died of blight. In the sunshine he read his Plutarch, pacing back and forth with a courtly bearing that led the townspeople to call him "Cayuga Chief."

THE VALUE OF
AN OTTER'S HOLE

ELIJAH Alford, first justice of the peace in Liberty Township, lost $3 to an otter. To be precise, Squire Alford lost the money to Hiram Messenger, on account of an otter. Here's how:

On his way to Garrett's Mill with a sack of corn, Messenger flushed an otter from its hiding place in the bullrushes. He dropped the corn and chased this valuable pelt to its hole, which he plugged with a stone. Then he went to hunt up a shovel, calculating how he would spend the money he expected to get for the hide. Over the hill came Thatcher F. Conant with a spade on his shoulder. "Could I borrow that shovel?" said Messenger. "Whatever for?" said Conant. After the explanation about the otter's hole, Conant bought the rights to it for a promise of $3.

Messenger proceeded to get his corn ground. Conant easily found the hole, but found neither hide nor hair of any otter. "There was one in it when I sold it to you," Messenger insisted, and he demanded his payment. "If there was any such otter in the first place," Conant replied, "it vamoosed before ever you saw me or my shovel." And he refused to pay.

Hence Justice of the Peace Elijah Alford heard the case of Messenger *v.* Conant "for the value of an otter's hole." Squire Alford inspected the hole and found it to be a true enough burrow all right. And the stone plugged it up nicely. But whether an otter had ever been domiciled there, before or after the sale of rights, was a puzzler. In the end he awarded $1.50 to Hiram Messenger and therefore shortened Thatcher Conant's promise by the same amount. Both men promptly gave notice of an appeal, the one for the recovery of his extra $1.50, the other for relief from all charges. To avoid a new suit, and a second inspection of the otter's hole, Squire Alford paid Messenger the $3, and that was that.

THE MULTIPLICATION
OF WOOL

ENCRUSTED with twigs and cockleburrs, the sheep drifted by her door like a filthy tide. Mrs. Josiah Ward watched the drove pass, imagining each animal a walking blanket, a four-legged shirt. "How much you want for the sheep?" she asked the drover. Glancing at the rickety cabin, the man answered, "More than you've got."

She hurried indoors, then returned blinking into the daylight. "I have a stocking here," she said. At sight of the lumpy sock dangling from her fist the drover stopped his herd. "These here sheep are bespoke by Timothy Culver," he told her, eyeing the sockful of money. "He'll only let them eat poisonweed down by the creek and kill theirselves like he did the last ones," she said, taking from the stocking a handful of coins which she had brought with her from Connecticut for the single purpose of buying sheep. The deal was swiftly made, and she owned eight of the ragamuffin beasts.

That night, while the sheep mulled about in a log pen, she sheared them all in her dreams. Come morning, she found two of them slaughtered by wolves. She gathered the wool that had been strewn about the carcasses, washed out the cockleburrs and blood, carded and spun it. She would weave it later into cloth for breeches. Every night afterward she locked the surviving sheep in her kitchen, where the three older children slept.

Despite her care, one of the sheep ate poisonweed, swelled up and burst. She salvaged that fleece, as well as the fleece from two others which had broken through ice on the creek. Of the three sheep still alive in the spring, only one was a dam. But she bore young, which in due time bore their own young, until Mrs. Ward owned an entire flock, all sprung from that stocking full of Connecticut coins. Her wheel spun through the day, her loom clacked into the night. Her family dressed warmly.

HUNT

AMID fiendish squawking, eight chickens disappeared in the night. This was the last outrage. Two of the hens belonged to Colonel Caleb Punderson, who had already lost six sheep, eight hogs, four cows, and nineteen chickens to the ravenous night beasts. The colonel had led raids upon rattlesnake dens, marching every springtime among the ledges with his ax and rifle, until the yellow rattler and the black were both extinguished. Now he wanted to exterminate the bears, wolves, wildcats, and mountain lions that were slaughtering his livestock.

Accordingly, on a November Saturday in 1822, when animal legs were stiff with cold, he posted armed men around the borders of the township. At the cry of a horn, echoed from bugler to bugler, the men waded forward, driving game before them toward the center of the township. When the ring had tightened to some half mile in diameter, Punderson gave the signal to fire, and the men shot everything that moved.

After the thrashing stopped they waded forward once again, squeezing the circle, shooting every beast they

"Punderson gave the signal to fire . . ."

flushed from the thickets and swamps. At last the circle closed, and the men faced one another over the carcasses of twenty-two bears, seven wolves, one hundred three deer, two mountain lions, one wildcat, plus turkeys and countless smaller game.

The meat and hides were divided among the hunters. The small game was left for the dogs. That night, while men scraped fat from bears strung up to bleed, while women plucked turkeys, there were no sounds of dying hogs or chickens, and from the woods came only the sound of dogs gnawing upon the bones of squirrels.

WHAT THEY TOLD
ABOUT THE BEASTS

HERE is what they told about the beasts: On the slate ledges above Justin Eddy's place the men killed seventy-two yellow rattlesnakes on one Sunday. The largest rattler was hauled out and tormented for an hour with sharpened poles. At last the creature clamped its fangs into one of the sticks and its venom ascended, by actual measure, twenty-two inches through the pores of the wood.

The last deer ever to be surprised grazing on the town square of Carthage was a sixteen-point buck, stoned to death by a gang of boys in 1819.

When Miss Sally Taylor lost her way one night in the Muskingum Woods, the wolves soon closed round, and she concluded all was up with her. The horse wanted to bolt, but she kept tight hold on the bridle. Then she crept under its quivering belly and sheltered there all night, screeching at the wolves when they drew too near.

Late one evening Lemuel Chapman lost his way in the woods east of his house while searching for cows. Afraid of getting further lost, he climbed a tree to spend the night. Not long after, he could hear his son Joel down below, saying, "Well, I guess the wolves have got Daddy." Whereupon the old man sang out, "I'll get you when I come down," thereby scaring son Joel nearly senseless.

In 1808 Kate Briggs met a bear on the path leading to the woodpile and in a fair and square fight she killed it with her ax, the wives of Ben and Gib McDaniels acting as umpires.

Upon hearing a ruckus from her sheep pen, Eunice Sheldon grabbed a rail off the fence and went to investigate. What she at first thought to be a large dog gutting one of her ewes turned out to be a panther. Without so much as yelling for her husband, she brained the great lion, and later made a lap rug from it.

The mother of Squire Crocker stopped her spinning wheel one day in 1820, to see why it was making such a curious noise. She soon heard the rattler a-buzzing beneath the floorboards. Her son routed his snakeship out and staved in its head. The length of it was six feet, two inches.

And so the war with the beasts simmered on. Within five decades after the first white settlers arrived in Pilgrim County, these animals were extinct in all that territory: elk, panther, wolf, bear, wildcat, beaver, black and yellow rattlesnakes, bald eagle.

THE INDIANS WIN
ANOTHER ONE

IT was rare for any merchant to be so badly fooled that he wept. For Heman Ovatt it was more than rare. He would have told you it was impossible. He made his living by fooling others, especially Indians, in the store he kept a mile south of Hudson.

One day an aged Seneca squaw, with hands and face swollen by gout, hobbled up to Ovatt's store leading a horse she wanted to swap. The trader looked her over first, and then her horse. She seemed demented, with slits for eyes, as if the pressure of swelling in her head had choked her brains. The horse appeared to be a soldier's mount, likely stolen, a fine black stallion with taut haunches, sound legs, teeth that had worn evenly, and clear eyes that stared ahead without twitching. The flesh on the ribs bespoke good feeding; the sleek black coat, good breeding.

The mount would fetch three Indian ponies from a certain captain at Fort Defiance, Ovatt calculated. So, after running his hands over the stallion's legs, and walking him around the lot in front of the store, he offered the woman one Indian pony in exchange. Only one? she demanded, through lips so puffy they could barely part. But he will take so much feed to keep, Ovatt complained. I have two sons, she said, holding up the appropriate number of fingers. Two sons, two sons. The merchant watched her eyes peering steadily at him through the slits in her bloated face. He laid his hand on the stallion's chest. Very well, he agreed, two ponies.

Within a week the stallion began stumbling dizzily about the lot. Presently the beast keeled over, its belly swollen. A party of Seneca braves arrived in time to see Ovatt stooping over his dead horse. Tears rolled down the trader's face. The Senecas never forgot. They named him Coppaqua, meaning "to weep." And every time they passed his store they cast stones onto a pile beside his door, as they cast stones upon the graves of their defeated enemies.

THE CHARACTER OF HOGS

YOU could take a humble Massachusetts barnyard hog, turn it loose to forage in the backwoods of Ohio, and inside of twelve months it would show up with bristles along its spine, blood on its gums, and mayhem in its eyes. Come upon a herd of them while they were rooting for acorns, and you were liable to lose a foot, or a dog. No matter how pure the strain of pig you brought with you, after a few years of mixing with backwoods swine it would emerge long-snouted and roach-backed as any boar.

This disturbed Christian Cackler's sense of order. Hogs had no more business reverting to savagery than men did. Cackler still bathed and prayed and wore clothes, even though he had long since left Amherst, Massachusetts, for Aurora, Ohio. He expected no less stability of character from his swine.

What to do? First shut them off from wild beasts with a log barn and rail fence. Then feed them only corn and silage, no more forest food. Breed them carefully, always selecting the fattest and most peaceable. Within a few years, while his neighbors let their own swine roam wild, Cackler produced hogs that were docile as any sheep. They would lie in the mud from one feeding to the next and could put on two hundred fifty pounds of flesh in ten months.

These new hogs were obedient meat manufactories, with no taint of woods left in them. You could set a yawping baby in front of one (as Cackler did for an experiment) and the pig would not so much as bare its teeth.

At the first Pilgrim County agricultural fair in 1825, Cackler's swine won him the $4 prize for livestock breeding. When his herd grew large enough for marketing, he found the beasts were too lazy to walk the hundred miles to Pittsburgh. Forced to butcher his ponderous hogs in Aurora, Cackler cured as much of the pork as he could, and peddled the rest door to door. Neighbors who bought some complained of the fat.

THE SWELLING AND
SHRINKING OF THE WORLD

IN one issue of his newspaper, Le Grand Byington commonly publicized more threats to the Republic than most people could worry about in a lifetime. There were the Masons, of course, and the Pope, plus slaveholders, whiskey distillers, Boston merchants, tax officials, and army surveyors, not to mention the Indians or the post office.

Life in New York had taught Byington vigilance, long before he hauled his press and type and perspicuity out to Indiana. Every manner of scofflaw and conspirator you cared to name could be turned up within five minutes in the streets of New York City. That place was past saving; but perhaps Indiana could still be salvaged. Byington founded his *Great Western Public Advertiser and Family Visitor* there in 1825, in an attempt to defend the frontier against the eastern infection.

"We are opposed to all secret combinations and associations, under whatever plausible character," he announced in his first issue. For motto he quoted Mr. Thomas Jefferson: "Opposition to Tyranny Is Obedience to God."

Catholics or Knights Templars, he didn't care who they were—if they met in secret, they were a menace. Slavers or bankers or ship's captains—anybody who lorded it over another human being was an enemy of Le Grand Byington.

When his smeared four-column sheet first hit the dirt roads of southern Indiana, people stopped in their tracks to read it, or to hear someone else read it. The day before, their lives had been wordless, and the world had stopped somewhere near the edges of their cornpatch. Now with this first newspaper, suddenly the world swelled out to include Washington and London, plus troubles enough to inspire unease in heaven.

For $2 per year, in advance, or $2.50 at year's end, citizens could feast themselves weekly on the prose of Le Grand Byington. As the conspiracies became more involved, so did the editor's sentences. The day eventually came when no one in the territory except the Congregational minister could make heads or tails of the reports, and even he was forced to specialize in those dealing with the wickedness of Catholics. Subscriptions dropped from eight hundred fourteen to six by the time Jackson defeated Adams in the election of 1828. Convinced that the eastern infection had caught up with him, Byington decided to move his press and *Great Western Public Advertiser and Family Visitor* to Illinois. The world in the minds of his readers shrank overnight.

BONES

EVERY time Jeremiah Needham turned his plow to avoid the burial mounds in his field, he regretted the waste of soil. One spring therefore he decided to scatter the mounds with a shovel. His spade soon clacked against bone. Being a superstitious man, he brushed the dirt away cautiously, eventually disclosing a human skeleton some seven feet tall. In the jawbone there were three teeth of silver; on the wrists, bracelets of copper; in the cavity of the chest, the iridescent bits of a seashell.

I am a rich man, Needham thought, loading the bones into his wagon for carrying to town, where he would consult with the teacher and doctor. As he pulled into the main street, first children and then adults drew alongside the wagon, ogling the silver-toothed skull, hefting the massive thigh bones. "That come out of your mounds?" someone asked. Needham drove without answering to the doctor's office. After wiring a few of the bones together and hanging them upon a stand, the doctor whistled. Needham had uncovered a giant.

Led to the doctor's by a trail of rumors, the teacher

peered at the skeleton in amazement. This, he declared, was one of the ancient people who had raised the mounds of earth and stone, dug quarries into beds of flint, fashioned the shapes of gigantic alligators and snakes with red clay. This dangling skeleton had belonged to a race whose trade routes had extended to the Atlantic Ocean, to the Gulf of Mexico, and all the way up the St. Lawrence to the northern seas.

Would the state pay for any more skeletons he dug up? Needham wanted to know. Technically, the teacher answered, the mounds were already state property, protected as ancient relics. Like hell, Needham declared, and drove his wagon and his skeleton back to the farm—where he found half a hundred townspeople shoveling wildly in his field. By the time he fetched his rifle from the cabin, the diggers had fled.

But that night as he lay scheming how to use his money, he heard the clack-clack of shovels against bone. Whenever he carried his lantern and gun to one part of the field, the sounds of shoveling would arise from another. After seventeen nights the mounds were leveled, and the gigantic skeletons were gone.

WHITE MAN'S GAME

THE Indians did not know what to make of Joshua Ewing's sheep. The beasts were too small to ride, too lazy for game, too stupid for company. What does white man want them for? Their fur, Ewing explained. Fleece, wool. Make britches and blankets. White man take our meadows to raise blankets? Not take your meadows, Ewing replied. Only four little sheep.

By springtime the four had become seven, and the Indians' puzzlement gave way to fear. Eat much grass, the Indians protested. Not so much, Ewing answered, only seven little sheep. And then sixteen, then forty, and within a few years the Indians could not cross their hunting grounds without stumbling over one of the sluggish animals. Ewing traded his surplus sheep to neighbors for axheads, barrels, goosedown, seed.

Soon the wildflowers vanished from clearings, nibbled down to the roots by free-ranging herds. No more yellow sprays of wood sorrel, no more blue-eyed grasses, no more purple spiderworts. When deer ambled into meadows at dusk they found nothing but stubble and thorns. Game

"The Indians meandered through their deserted
hunting grounds like spirits of the unburied dead."

drifted west, into the deeper woods, where there were no white men or sheep. Wolves followed the deer, and so did rabbits, raccoons, bears. Gnawed and scuffed by sheep, hilltops lost their topsoil, turning the rivers black. In the villages every bite of food gritted with dust. The Indians meandered through their deserted hunting grounds like spirits of the unburied dead.

Earth follow deer away, the Indians complained. Your sheep eat all the grasses, no roots keep earth here. But the white men had multiplied almost as quickly as their sheep, and they no longer parleyed.

The Indians found that the sheep died easily, from an arrow at the base of the neck or from a stone blow to the head. At first they scattered their kills, eating every last shred of mutton, burying the hide and bones. The white men had too many animals to count.

Come another spring, and the deer not returned, and the rivers still running black with soil, the Indians began killing every sheep they could find. Graceless beasts, too stupid ever to stop gnawing the grasses, the slaughtered sheep rose in stinking piles when the cavalry arrived from Fort Sandusky. The sheep soon multiplied to their old numbers again, and more, but never the Indians.

OF TEETH AND
TRANSPORTATION

JABEZ Gilbert lost his teeth driving a four-horse stage-coach between Pittsburgh and Cleveland. Stumps, rocks, and gullies rattled them loose. On the twice-weekly runs delivering mail and people, his tailbone grew familiar with every bump in the road. Calling it a road, as the politicians did, was a generosity. The only clear stretches followed the great Indian trail. When Gilbert hit those stretches he let out the horses and made his rackety stage fairly fly.

Once in a while he would lollop over a hill and see a redskin lurking away back in the bushes, waiting for him to pass. Pass he did, and in a hurry, for he prided himself on never being more than eight hours off schedule. Business had to go forward on time, even if it cost him his teeth. What the Indians could still be doing, padding back and forth along their old trail, was a puzzle to him. So far as that went, he wasn't sure what kind of savage trade could ever have drawn enough of them a-walking to pack this road so hard in the first place.

There was plenty of trade among white people, he knew

that for a fact. Two horses and a wagon bouncing once a week between Pittsburgh and Cleveland used to carry all the traffic there was. By 1826, Gilbert had to get a proper stagecoach, add a second team of horses, and increase his runs to twice weekly, in order to keep up with the flow of letters and bodies. Most of it was heading west.

Often he would accept a bushel of wheat or two pounds of lead shot in exchange for a parcel—that was how badly some people wanted their mail. But other folks (and comfortable-off ones at that) would look at the envelope he'd brought them, see it was from an uncle or preacher back in Delaware, say, and they'd refuse to pay the postage. So half the mail would end up in the dead-letter office.

Twice a year the newspaper would print a list of unde-livered mail, and on it would be the names of prominent citizens, too cheap to pay for news from back east. The only piece of mail Jabez Gilbert ever looked for from that direction was the packet from Boston containing his made-to-order teeth, which, when they finally arrived, were in several more pieces than their maker could possi-bly have intended. After Gilbert glued them back to-gether, they fit tolerably well, but he could not wear them when he was driving.

LOVE-CROSSED CARPENTER

IF you wanted carpentry work done in that part of the Ohio Valley, you hired Nathan Muzzy. He was the best man with wood in the territory, but he refused all payment for his labors except bed and board. While he fashioned wainscot for the parlor or a banister for the stair, you had to listen to him tell about his misfortunes in love.

Everyone heard the same story, which he elaborated by the hour as wood shavings flew. He had graduated from Yale College, which was a rare enough feat. Even more rare, as a young minister he had received the gift of tongues, speaking to crowds of thousands in the towns back east. Then one night at a camp meeting while he addressed the multitudes, his gaze lit upon the face of a woman in the audience, and he could not look away. He could speak to no one but her. The crowd shuffled out grumbling before he finished his sermon, and that was the end of his career as a preacher.

He followed the woman home to her father's place. She would have nothing to do with him until he proved his love by building her a house. When the dwelling was finished she demanded furniture. And when Muzzy had turned the last spindle of the last chair, she married a New Haven lawyer, with whom she moved into the bridal house.

From that day forward Muzzy had meandered westerly, raising a cabin here or a barn there, paneling a room, carving children's toys. In every lodging he retold his story. By the time he reached Ohio he was in rags and his spine was bent. The only sturdy things about him were the hands and voice.

No one could persuade him to take money, or to linger after his work was done. Between jobs he ate berries. People told of overhearing him in the woods recounting his woes in the same entranced voice—and in the same words—as he had used in their parlors.

When he was found frozen one December near the pond that was later named after him, his body a rack of bones, the local people buried him. On his last carpentry job Muzzy had been overheard to sing out, "God be praised, the Devil's raised, the world rolls round in water." What he meant by that, no one knew.

THE WANDERING OF
LAKE ERIE

A MOS Spafford was so exasperated by the official rambling of Lake Erie that he addressed a letter to the Governor. Every map published, he wrote, moves the lake twenty miles east or forty-seven miles north, while I'm standing here on the shore knowing it hasn't budged an inch.

The Governor replied that he could make no sense of the surveyors' reports himself. Every landmark seemed to be scuttling about, Lake Ontario along with Erie, the Cuyahoga River along with Mount Misery and the Great Black Swamp. But the latest map, Spafford complained, had delivered fourteen by seventy-two miles of Ohio into the hands of Michigan, including his own farm. That got a rise out of the Governor, who could bear to have his creeks moved but not his lands diminished.

So he ordered a surveying party to settle the boundary with Michigan once and for all, before some new map maker delivered over Cleveland or Toledo. For leader of the party he chose Amos Spafford, who knew nothing about surveying but who could tell where a lake was when he saw one. After harvest was in, Spafford assumed command of the vagabond surveyors, who were muddy to their armpits from wading swamps. No sooner were their tripods set up, however, than a band of Michigan settlers swooped down upon them with beanpoles and pitchforks and routed them back into Ohio.

At Spafford's request the Governor sent militiamen to accompany the next expedition, which was attacked by an even larger contingent of militia from Michigan. Whereupon the Governor declared war, and war between the states there would have been if the federal marshals had not turned up with their guns cocked. At the court hearing over the boundary dispute Amos Spafford testified concerning the location of Lake Erie and the whereabouts of his own land, and was believed.

BORDER WAR

IN a fashion unbecoming to a man in his position, Governor Mason of Michigan marched his troops upon Toledo, where they robbed melon patches and chicken coops, and kicked in the door of the house belonging to Major Stickney, whom they spirited away as prisoner of war. This proved to be a mistake, since Stickney's wife pursued the Michigan forces back across the border, catching up with them at a ford of the Raisin River, where she delivered the Governor in the presence of his troops a tongue-lashing which he would still remember wincingly in his old age.

The prisoner of war was returned. But Mrs. Stickney refused to budge until the Governor had paid her $27.13 in compensation to the people of Toledo for melons stolen and nerve-racked chickens.

Hearing of the skirmish, Governor Lucas of Ohio called out his own troops, crossed the border at Toledo and ransacked the whiskey still of Temperance, taking as prisoner Colonel Vinton, a doddering veteran of the Revolution. There was nothing doddering about Mrs. Vinton, however, who followed the Governor back into Ohio and, not content to deliver a tongue-lashing, crept upon him in the night and stabbed him in the thigh with a paring knife.

That, for all practical purposes, ended the war. Ambassadors duly arrived from Washington to negotiate matters. Both governors were anxious to avoid future raids, with or without prisoners of war. Land was swapped between Michigan and Ohio, entire creekbeds and villages changed statehood overnight.

In three days the new border was drawn straight as a prairie railroad track, and the troops retired to their farms, the ambassadors to Washington. Afterward Mrs. Vinton hugged Mrs. Stickney, advising her to use a paring knife next time, because it saves breath.

SLAVES NO MORE

JOHN and Harriet escaped into Ohio from Huntington, West Virginia, with only their black skins and their Christian names. Passing from one abolitionist household to another, the fugitives stole northward. Near Columbus they met General William Steadman, late U.S. consul to Santiago, who ushered them as far as the village of Randolph, in Portage County. Ely Meade and Oliver Brainerd hired the two runaways to work in their sawmill there, put them up in their own attic, and vouched for the couple's safety.

By and by, the man who called himself their owner—one Mitchell from West Virginia—discovered the whereabouts of John and Harriet. On a rainy Saturday in May 1847, two of Mitchell's sons drove up to the Randolph Hotel and engaged lodgings. On their wagon rested a man-sized cage, crudely lashed together out of beechwood poles. Later that night these two Mitchells were seen making their way down the steam-mill road, backed up by ten Ohio River boatmen.

Word reached Meade and Brainerd, who padlocked the

door into the attic, and met the would-be kidnappers at the front gate. The two millers took along axes to aid in the parley. Before this conversation was over, upwards of seventy-five citizens, of all ages and sexes, surrounded the kidnappers with a thicket of shovels and pitchforks.

Presently the Mitchell sons decided they did not want to claim John and Harriet after all, and the boatmen decided that running rapids was safer than fetching slaves out of Ohio. So this delegation of kidnappers was escorted back to the hotel, guarded through the night, and sent packing next morning. Two spies made sure the kidnappers crossed back over the river. The beechwood cage was dismantled and the wood used for beanpoles.

Hatred for Ohio abolitionists in general—and for the militant souls of Randolph in particular—mounted one notch higher in West Virginia. A week after this raid John and Harriet were married, with all the leading citizens of the county in attendance. Randolph, they called themselves, John and Harriet Randolph.

COURTHOUSE

THE first courthouse in Pilgrim County suffered a history eventful enough for any dozen buildings. The Pickawillany brothers built it, in exchange for the return of several parcels of real estate which their father, in a weak moment, had donated to the county. It was two stories high, forty feet long, and all of oak timbers hewn eighteen inches square. Every opening was grated with iron. The outside was covered with two-inch oak planks secured with hickory pegs. Upstairs were the courtroom and debtors' cells; downstairs, the jail and sheriff's quarters. Every other building in Roma looked flimsy by comparison. That was in 1810.

Nobody was led out from there to be hanged until 1813. By 1815 the jail had acquired such a remarkable stink that judges were refusing to sit in the chambers upstairs. So court was moved to Amzi Atwater's house, across the street and upwind. Meanwhile the jail was springing leaks. Rust had got the better of the iron hinges and window bars. Only a lazy prisoner would be kept indoors for long. Tossing uneasily on their featherticks, the

"Every other building in Roma looked
flimsy by comparison."

citizens of Roma decided to hire the Pickawillany brothers to build a more formidable jail.

The old building thenceforth went into decline. In 1826 the Roma *Bugle and Home Companion* was moved to comment upon the derelict courthouse as follows: "Pilgrim County can boast, on the score of public buildings, nothing but a shell, which is alternately occupied by bipeds and quadrupeds, and which, from its dilapidated state, is equally easy of access to both—and in which, we may at different times hear the preachers of the Gospel, the expounders of the law, and the birch of the schoolmaster, and consequently the squalls of the children, the squealing of pigs, and the bleating of sheep."

In 1829 the woebegone building was sold to General Samuel Harris, who moved it to his own land for a barn. It was next sold to Merts and Riddle's factory, where it became a soap manufactory. Then it went, timber by timber, to James Clark & Company, who converted it into a carriage shop.

By mid-century the courthouse had changed occupations seven times more, passing through the hands of tanners, wheelwrights, and saloonkeepers along the way. The oak timbers simply would not wear out. Long after the Pickawillany brothers had crossed the great divide, the former courthouse of Pilgrim County—then employed as a hog shed—burned down. That was in 1871.

ICE MOUNTAINS AND
HAIRY ELEPHANTS

THE deep gouges in the sandstone out front of Palmyra Wilson's store set everyone who saw them to pondering. They were the right shape and depth for furrows; but not even the new steel-tipped plows would cut through stone. Some of the old people spoke of angels landing there in the long-ago days, when flights from heaven were common as grass. Children explained the gouges by reference to giants and falling stars. But people who had their full ration of sense eventually gave up all attempt at explanation, and accepted the furrowed sandstone for what it was—one of God's mysteries.

When the government surveyor came to run the township boundaries, however, he stood long over those gouges, consulted his compass, and announced that a glacier had carved these marks. No one who lived within a day's walk of Palmyra Wilson's store had ever heard of a glacier. So, for anyone who was interested, the government surveyor drew pictures in the dirt and gestured with his arms to describe the mountain of ice that had swept over this country long ago.

Mountain of ice? Skidding down from the north? Driving boulders before it? The listeners spat in the dirt beside his illustrations, unconvinced.

Not only glaciers, the surveyor continued, eager to enlighten, but Lake Erie once spread over all these lands and away down south of here, a regular ocean. And not only oceans and ice, he explained, but terrible lizards taller than barns, and horses smaller than dogs, and hairy elephants. By the time his lecture arrived at elephants, only children and old people still listened. They at least *wished* what he said were true. Palmyra Wilson believed none of it. But he did put a shed over the furrowed sandstone, and charged a penny to anyone who wanted a look.

THE BOY WHO
NURSED CLEVELAND

B Y the time Cleveland had grown too large to spit across, it began to suffer town problems—bankers, judges, horse thieves, whores. Worst of all were the fever and ague. Nob Stiles watched his father come down with it, then all nine of his brothers and sisters, then his mother, then everyone in the neighboring cabins. He kept waiting for the sickness to flare in his own joints, the shakes to possess his limbs. But the fever never lit in him.

A sister died, another sister, then a brother. The only life left in his father was in the twitching eyes. And all day long it was: "Nob fetch the bucket, Nob poke the fire, Nob go scrub your brother who's beshat himself." Better fever, Nob told himself when he lay down at last to sleep. Come sweet ague.

A morning soon arrived when he was the only resident of Cleveland as old as thirteen years of age who could stand on his feet. Now filthy coverlets and slopbuckets had to be left stinking; there was no time for anything but carrying food and water. He fed corn mush to his family. What was left he delivered to the neighbors. When that was gone he carved away at the salt pork, dragged sacks of turnips and carrots from the root cellar. When he heard a baby squawking he laid it on its mother, for whatever good the child could get out of the flaccid breasts.

His own mother whispered to him from the heap of children and quilts where she lay shivering. Set the lard on to heat, she told him. Pound that meal as fine as you can get it. Now knead it, that's right, add water, add salt, make the little patties like you've seen me do. And so Nob Stiles baked johnnycakes for Cleveland. Wrapped in a tow sack, the cakes stayed warm from cabin to cabin. When the feverish throats could not swallow, he crumbled the bread into water, into milk or whiskey, into whatever there was a jug of, and he spoon-fed the victims.

Come sweet ague, he kept praying, deliver me from these labors. But the disease still passed him by, and after two months it relinquished everyone in Cleveland whom it had not killed.

THE PHILOSOPHICAL
COBBLER

THE grandfather of General (later President) Ulysses
S. Grant tanned hides and cobbled shoes in Pilgrim
County. Neighbors knew him simply as Noah Grant, the
close-tongued man to whom you took your skins for curing, from whom you bought your moccasins or, if well-
to-do, your boots.

For a long time no one expected him to become the father, let alone grandfather, of anybody. He was too spar-
ing of words ever to put together a speech long enough to
qualify as a marriage proposal. Contrary to the predictions
of Roma's gossips, however, he did marry. In due time he
fathered a son, Jesse, who fathered a son, Ulysses, who
helped lead a multitude of other sons, both Union and
Confederate, into premature graves.

Although he lived by tanning the hides of murdered
animals, Noah did not like killing, and never fired a gun.
Skins heaped all around him while he worked: bear, otter,
marten, deer, the reeking wildcat and fox, panther and
wolf, the sumptuous mink. The animal kingdom seemed
to have shed its collective coat in his tanning shack. The

longer he worked among hides, the more silent he became, as if the tannic acid were curing him of speech.
Dumb beast among dumb beasts, the neighbors said.

In his silence, Noah never left off musing. Perhaps a
way could be found to skin the animals without killing
them, as sheep were sheared for their wool? Perhaps the
deer and panthers could be bred so that each animal
would bear a dozen thicknesses of skin, and thus fewer
need be killed? Or maybe some vegetable could be trained
to produce fur instead of fruit? Noah became, in short, a
philosopher.

While his knife scraped fat from a raccoon skin, or his
needle pierced the hide of an otter, he contemplated the
world's secret equations: Nine bearskins would buy you a
rifle, forty-three would buy a horse; between eighty-five
and one hundred deer would get you a yoke of oxen;
mink was worth about the same, inch per inch, as calico;
for one muskrat you could get stinking drunk on rye
whiskey, and for a panther you could stay that way a
week. There was occult meaning in these equations. If
you thought about them long enough, the grandfather of
U. S. Grant was persuaded, you could deduce the paths of
stars and the cause of wars.

FREEING THE WATERS

MIASMA lurked upon the still waters—every citizen of Mercer County was persuaded of that. Their children came down with fever in the muggy days of August, their cattle slumped over, and their sheep ran mad. The government engineer had said nothing of malaria when he argued them into selling land to build the reservoir. Land itself was cheap, he had told them. Farms could be bought farther west. But without this reservoir there could be no canal from Lake Erie to the Ohio River, and without the canal there could be no progress, could there? Did they want their state to remain forever a pathless wilderness while the rest of the nation was carved up by roads of water and stone and steel?

So they sold—at a stiff price. And they hired themselves out to girdle thousands of acres of trees where the water would spread, wondering as they swung their axes who would harvest all that timber. No one did. The trees stood there, doomed and waiting.

The men of Mercer County worked as shovelers and mule drivers, raising walls of earth to dam their valley. On a day chosen by the engineer, the waters of the Muskingum River were admitted into this earthen trap, and the girdled trees were standing there still. Few of the men and none of the women could bear to watch the waters rising over farms they had worked. The children turned away as water drowned their playfields. Treetops lifted above the murky waters like a dwarf forest.

Then came the fevers. Poisonous vapors—miasma—rose from the stagnant waters and seeped into barns and cabins, into bellies and lungs.

When her second cow died and her daughter fell sick, Shirley Hatch seized a shovel and went to visit the neighbors. Soon one hundred and fifty residents of the county were digging a breach in the embankment. The reservoir had bled dry into river valleys farther south before any shoveler was arrested. And no grand jury in the county could be found to draw up a bill of indictment, not even against Shirley Hatch, whose daughter survived and whose hands showed no blisters from the spade.

BROKEN-BOOTED
CANAL BUILDER

HOW anyone wearing boots as broken as those of Captain Hebediah Dumest could walk a line straight enough to lay out a canal was a good question. But in 1829, when bills chartering the Pennsylvania and Ohio Canal Company were finally passed, he was the only U.S. Army engineer still residing above ground in Pilgrim County. So he was hired to survey the eighty-two-mile route, broken boots and all.

Captain Dumest, who found his name a cause for regret, found his agreement to survey the canal an even greater one. Every farmer between Akron, Ohio, and Newcastle, Pennsylvania, wanted the channel to pass through his farm, and offered arguments ranging from peach brandy to revolvers why it should. Every town within fifty miles of the proposed route held meetings, where otherwise sober citizens whooped it up for the canal in rambunctious fashion. The captain enjoyed little peace.

Malarial swamps, glacial moraines, and outcroppings of adamantine slate further complicated his choice of route.

"Captain Dumest bought himself a new pair of boots which he soon wore out . . ."

The surveying maps he lugged from camp to camp began to resemble illustrations of cobwebs. His boots leaked. Finally in 1835 the survey was completed, and the commissioners, after haggling over a few jigs and jogs in the route, approved it. Several of these gentlemen bought stock in the canal company with bribes they had received for favoring one town or another. Captain Dumest bought himself a new pair of boots, which he soon wore out by supervising the digging of the channel.

Five years and $913,000 later, the last shovelful of dirt was heaved out of the ditch, all the feeder lakes were loosed into the channel, and the Ohio and Pennsylvania Canal joined the ranks of artificial rivers. First boat through from the East was the *Mohawk,* carrying a band of musicians who played a concert eighty-two miles long. First boat through in the opposite direction was the *Ohio City,* freighted with ashes, whiskey, and fish. Dumest rode aboard all the way to Beaver, Pennsylvania, and then he rode back. Towns celebrated everywhere along the route.

The canal he had surveyed churned with boats until 1856, when the newly opened Cleveland and Mahoning Valley Railroad stole its traffic. For $30,000 the railroad bought the canal. Standing once again in broken boots, the captain watched them drain it, lay tracks, and run trains through his glorious ditch.

HEALING WATERS

EVEN if Moses Byxbe had never heard of your ail-ment, he would swear that his white sulphur waters should cure it. As for curing the familiar maladies, such as bilious derangements and scrofulous affections, he would sell you his spring water with a money-back guarantee. If you were not healed in a fortnight, all you had to do to retrieve your money was hunt through half the Ohio Valley until you found him—that is, if whatever ailed you had not already killed you.

For Byxbe kept moving on, ladling water from his vat on the horsecart into the waiting cups and milk pails of those who came to him in search of health. Many came. Out of the woods limped every manner of bodily and spiritual infirmity. Those who could not walk were borne forth on stretchers, teeth gnashing or mouths sagging open. This daily sight so moved Byxbe that for nine weeks he stopped selling his waters, which he knew to be harmless—and useless. But the sufferers hunted him out in his village, drawn there by miraculous stories.

And so he refilled his vat at the hydrosulphurous spring

and creaked forth again into the roadways, only now he gave his water away, begging his own food. With each ladleful he laid his hand upon the victim's head and proclaimed, "Be made whole." Byxbe himself was hardly an inspiring sight, for his face was gaunt as a withered pumpkin, his mouth was a foul mire of rotted teeth, his back was warped from a life of lifting. And yet when he said, "Be made whole," his voice gritted with the determination of rockslides. His damp hand smelling of brimstone felt weighty with power upon the head.

Although he shriveled from month to month as if he were a pond whose dam had sprung a leak, he kept at his healing, and the afflicted everywhere hobbled after him with their needs, until the day he went to refill his vat at the spring and never came back.

SLANDER

HARRIET Perkins complained to the justice that Thankful Bissell had said something derogatory to her character. "What exactly did she say?" Squire Forward asked. But the good woman was not about to repeat so vile a statement. "Then how am I to know it was slanderous?" the justice inquired. "Because I'm here telling you so," said Harriet Perkins. This required some looking into.

Squire Forward took seriously his duties as justice of the peace, especially in the peacemaking end of them. In the case of Perkins *v.* Bissell he quickly established that the altercation had taken place on a Wednesday evening churchgoing. He further discovered that the two parties to the suit were longstanding enemies over rights to drinking water from Everlasting Spring.

On the night in question, Harriet Perkins had, by her own admission, prodded Thankful Bissell verbally on the subject of water rights. And Thankful Bissell, by all accounts, had put the English language to strenuous use in defending her side of the wrangle. Percisely where that language had touched upon the character of Harriet Perkins was a matter of debate. If Squire Forward was to believe the reports of all bystanders, then the character of this matron was left generally black-and-blue by the exchange. Some mentioned comparisons with hogs, others with Baptists; some noted references to dung; still others recollected mention having been made of historic harlots from various lands.

At last the justice was driven in his perplexity to ask Thankful Bissell herself what had transpired. "I said she was carrying on like she had Indian blood in her," Bissell readily confessed. True or not, Squire Forward decided, that observation was a shade too strong for announcement in public. So deciding, he fined Thankful Bissell one gallon of whiskey, plus 25 cents in costs.

THE INDIANS
LOSE IT ALL

AMONG the quills employed in defending the abused red man from the white, one of the ablest was that of the poet Jessamine Mooney. Newspapers featured her verses between the stock notices and hog reports. Ministers intoned her rhymes from the pulpit. Children recited them while picking elderberries or setting muskrat traps. The poetry of Jessamine Mooney and the mistreatment of Indians were two subjects never far separated in polite conversation around mid-century.

The poet herself would speak upon the topic for $3.50 plus coach fare. Any group who hired her received more than its money's worth. She would repeat the statement made by General Sam Houston, to the effect that there never had been an Indian war in which the white man was not the aggressor. She would haul out a map of the Ohio Valley, with the Indian words for rivers, counties, and towns left blank, and show you what a piebald-looking place it would be without all those savage names. She would recite you her verses in honor of the red man until the air thinned in the meeting hall.

Her lifetime project was to extol Indians in every poetical form employed since the time of Horace. By 1860 she had worked her way as far as the heroic couplets of Alexander Pope. She also aimed to include in a single elegy the name of every tribe that had ever so much as camped in the Ohio Valley. The latter effort was hindered by the difficulty of finding suitable rhymes for words such as Potawatomies, Piankeshaws, Kaskaskias, and Kickapoos. Sometimes a rhyme would come to her while she was in the middle of an oration, and she would be forced to break off her speech in order to mark it down.

The fewer the Indians who lingered in the valley, the more popular Jessamine Mooney's verses became. By 1863, when her elegy was finished, with rhymed couplets featuring the names of two hundred eleven tribes, a person could ride on a train from New York City to St. Louis and never pass within sight of Indian land.

WITHOUT REGARD
TO RACE

THE Underground Railroad would get you safely from Tennessee into Ohio, but the Angel Gabriel himself could not get you or your children into a white school. Better to have stopped in Kentucky, where the Quakers ran academies that took in white and colored people both. But Rebeccah Versailles had already reached Ashtabula County, Ohio, smack up against Lake Erie. She would never move south again, even if the Greek philosophers opened up a college down there specifically for black folks. The Quakers had petered out somewhere near Marietta. The other varieties of Christians did not hold with educating their children alongside former slaves. State law agreed.

When Versailles asked the trustees about enrolling her four children, they read her the Ohio statute of 1829, which spared black and mulatto persons from paying school tax and also barred them from attending white institutions. Colored people are to start their own, the trustees advised her. You get together with your people, build

"In exchange for her work, the schoolmaster
let her squat in one corner of the classroom ..."

a school, learn up your children in your own particular ways.

That was a hard task. So far as Versailles could discover, the nearest colored family was twenty-three miles away. Then teach them yourself, the trustees replied. Law is law. It sure is, Versailles agreed, it surely is.

She could not teach her children what she did not know. So she became a master at carving pens out of turkey quills and stitching foolscap sheets into copybooks. In exchange for her work, the schoolmaster let her squat in one corner of the classroom while his white students practiced their writing, sums, and spelling. Each night she would spoon into her children what she had gleaned during the day. They learned to write using the finest quill pens in Ashtabula County.

After seven winters of this, all four of them were set to become teachers. Before Rebeccah Versailles sent them away to the Quaker institute, she made them promise never to refuse to teach anybody, not any variety of body whatsoever, who honestly wanted to learn.

ONE OF THE
UNION DEAD

WHEN Abraham Lincoln was elected President, you could set cotton wool afire by holding it in the air between a Democrat and a Republican. There was that much partisan heat. But after news of the rebel attack on Fort Sumter reached the telegraph office in Roma, all division of party or religion quickly evaporated. The heat was reserved for Confederates, who were roasted in speech after heartfelt speech at the Roma town meeting on April 15, 1861. Every minister and businessman, every elected official from state senator to county fence-viewer spoke upon the virtues of union and the iniquities of rebellion.

John Haven listened to the speeches until his head felt like a bloated feed sack. Only thing that would relieve the pressure, he calculated, was killing a few dozen of the rebels.

Back in Euphrates Township his wife received the news with tight lips. No matter. He added his matched pair of mules to the parade of teams, wagons, banners, and martial bands that converged on the Roma Town Hall on April 18. By the time he arrived the hall was full. So he stood outside among the bonfires and listened to the speakers through the open windows. He could not make out much of the speeches themselves, but the shouts and huzzahs from the audience set his spine atingle. Since the Euphrates Township Martial Band was parked right beside him, he had no trouble joining in the patriotic songs.

He was among the first to volunteer. The term was three months, all the time it was expected to take for dispatching the rebels. Before he could escape with his unit to Camp Taylor, Haven had to spend a week frying in the angry gaze of his wife.

When he finally boarded the train for Cleveland, along with other members of the Roma Light Artillery Company, he was presented with a woolen blanket, a Navy six-shooter, and a silver badge. Engraved on the badge, just beneath the Union stars for which he was fighting, was his own name. His wife pinned it on him without saying a word. Three months later, after a skirmish with rebels on Scarey Creek, West Virginia, that badge was the only sure way of identifying John Buford Haven, who was the first man from Pilgrim County to die in the War of the Rebellion.

AMERICA IS ONE
LONG BLOODY FIGHT

WHAT could an old man do to preserve the Union? General Alphonso Roof wanted to know. He rose before the Roma town meeting on seventy-eight-year-old legs. Born in the last year of the Revolution to a man who died fighting the English, wounded at the Battle of Lake Erie in 1813, one arm twisted from an encounter with a bear, his face scarred from Indian fights, eyes squinted from five decades of plowing—the general stood before the people of Pilgrim County like a living archive of their history.

If heart were all that was needed, he would fight the rebels before supper. But his body just would not go anymore. Form a Home Guard, then, Judge Luther Day suggested. The audience cheered. A motion was passed empowering the general to do just that.

Enough boys and aged men joined him to form a respectable company. When it was discovered that some of the boys were actually girls in long breeches, General Roof said he would train them anyway, plus any other women who turned up. If the rebels invaded Ohio, he explained, everybody with a stout heart would be needed for defense—and women had about the stoutest hearts he had ever come across.

Since there were barely enough rifles to equip the regular militia, the Home Guard rehearsed for war carrying broomhandles and cornstalks. The general did not bother with marching or any of the other rigmarole inherited from Old World soldiering. He taught his recruits how to bush up in a clump of sumac and lay for the enemy with tomahawks. He taught the quickest boys and girls how to steal horses, on the chance that enemy cavalry might one day show up. Women and the sturdiest old men he instructed in the use of bowie knives, which had been made to his order by a Lebanon Township blacksmith. Into every house in the county he introduced a tiny sack of poison, to be dished out to occupying soldiers. Anyone who questioned these bloodthirsty preparations was told in heated Yankee English that the country had been won by fighting, made rich by fighting, and would damn well be kept in one piece by fighting. America is one long bloody fight, he explained, and don't you ever forget it.

The war kept General Roof alive, right up through Lee's surrender at Appomattox. By and by he died, without seeing the enemy again, without doubting that a new enemy was there, waiting.

THE MANNER OF
THEIR DYING

HERE is the manner of their dying:
Rachel Street, sent to fetch water from a spring, was killed by the falling of a tree.

Eliakim Goss drank too much tanglefoot whiskey while out surveying, and that dire liquid, plus the heat, finished him off.

Sticking with his gristmill during the April flood, George DePeyster was carried away with it down the Tuscarawas River.

Robert Wright, owner of a bad reputation, was found on the banks of Silver Creek with his throat cut from ear to ear.

While his brother was stealing honey, Israel Coe diverted a swarm of bees, which stung him to death.

Joshua Woodard's dam backed stagnant water for two miles up Breakneck Creek, which spawned malarial fevers, which did in a good many people thereabouts.

Asa Day ran afoul of Indians at a place called Stony Arabia on the Mohawk River.

Weary of being twitted by friends for never having

"Their dying was as various as their living . . ."

killed a deer, Enos Wadsworth swore he would bring one home or die in the attempt; he kept the latter part of his promise, by virtue of apoplexy, for he was discovered lying facedown in Gutty Swamp, with gun in hand and food in his pocket.

Orestes Hale brought the smallpox with him from Pittsburgh, shared it with neighbors, and died in feverish company.

Betsey Rogers thought the rattles were a toy, and crawled after the noisy snake that coiled beside her pallet.

On Muddy Lake, Zenas Carter was trying out the floating qualities of his new dugout canoe, which capsized, sending him to the bottom with his doeskin leggings.

Hauling a new grindstone from Coshocton over icy roads, Fairchild Hanks lost his wagon into a spin and lost himself beneath the stone.

When her stomach began to pain her, Anne Judson applied to Phoebe Hiram for an emetic, but was given arsenic by mistake, and so got beyond her stomach ailment.

John Dix applied to the Thompsonian doctors for relief from his heart problem, but his heart gave out before he completed their sweat treatment.

Samantha Frazer died from having her tooth extracted by the blacksmith.

Zebulon Tuttle went down a well after a cup he had dropped, and there he was overpowered by carbonic acid gas.

On her way to church, Jemima Palmer was surprised by

two calves jumping from the bushes, and she fell down on the spot, dead of wonder.

Their dying was as various as their living, such a compost of souls.

Exeter, New Hampshire
Eugene, Oregon
Bloomington, Indiana
1974–1983